A POLICEMAN GOT ME

A

JUST BAE

CONTENTS

PROLOGUE

Numb—the only word that can describe Detective Cynthia Jones. She's been sitting in the lobby of the precinct for hours senseless, unaware of how long.

"We'll take care of it. We're on it. We'll get to the bottom of this," Captain Rowland says escorting Cynthia to his patrol car. "We'll find those responsible. Let's get you home."

Just like that, her partner, Kenneth Miller was killed returning home from his shift earlier in the day. Flags were lowered at half staff around the city and the Mayor and Police Chief vowed to find his killers. With Kenneth's sudden departure, there wasn't even a sign to hold onto for a God's sake.

Cynthia's vision blurs; the Vogue magazines on her table are swimming around. This wasn't supposed to happen. She was so close, having the perfect partner on the force and was finally in love. Kenneth and Cynthia dated for close to six months after meeting on the force. He had proposed to her just two weeks ago, only to have him ripped away.

Cynthia curls up on the couch, drifting until someone knocks.

CHAPTER ONE

Six Weeks Ago

It's hard to remember a time Cynthia hasn't seen her former lover and partner, Detective Kenneth Miller go over his paycheck's deductions from his desk in the corner. This is Detective Cynthia Jones' first day back at work and she was called down to the coroner's office. As she walks down the hall, no one looks up at her. Kenneth's death is fresh in everyone's mind. The moment she reaches the door, the coroner yells "Poison!"

"That's it?" Cynthia looks on folding her arms. "You could have called me?"

"Despite having the latest technology in this room, I still prefer to meet face-to-face." The coroner looks at his papers and hands them to Cynthia. "We found thallium sulfate on the victim."

"What's that?"

"It's a tasteless, odorless, colorless liquid. The symptoms often mask as other symptoms and are almost impossible to detect."

"Are we talking about the jogger from the park? I thought you said he died from heart failure."

"That was my initial prognosis, Detective. Once, I got the body on my good old-fashioned table here, I found a bit more than what I was expecting."

"Sounds like you're fond of your work?"

"Yes, indeed."

Officer Al Sanchez walks in and

snatches the report from her. "Give me that back," Cynthia said pinching him.

"You already read it."

Cynthia snatches it back, "Thank you, Officer."

"How are you doing, Detective? It's good to see you."

"I'm better. I needed the time off. Thanks."

Cynthia smiles at coroner's handwriting. "This is some old-fashioned scribbling." She gives the papers back. "So. I guess the question is - who wanted this guy dead?"

"That's up your alley, Detective," Officer Al said.

"Of course, smart ass—Al. Let's go. I need to talk to Samuel's wife."

"After you, Ma'am."

———

"Tea, Detective?" Mrs. Janson said wiping her tears.

"No, thank you," Cynthia replies looking at the photos on the mantel.

"You, Officer?"

"No, thanks, ma'am," Al said flipping through his notes. Mrs. Janson puts the kettle on the table and goes inside the kitchen. Al turns to Cynthia, "I wouldn't if I were you."

"Wouldn't what?" Al looks toward the kitchen.

"Never mind. Hey, those photos on the mantle don't have Samuel in them."

"I didn't notice. I'm only an officer."

"Just stop it. Changing subjects, why don't you have some tea then?" Cynthia said. "Scared?"

"Better to live than die."

Cynthia pinches Al. "You're such a mess."

"One life to live."

"Funny! This is coming from the man

who talks bad about my favorite soap opera," Cynthia said moving closer to Al.

"I said I'd be more careful, remember? Almost got killed the last time I took charge."

"I'm glad. Would you have knocked the cup out of my hands if I were to take a sip?"

"I would have if I thought it was poisoned," Al said staring into Cynthia's eyes. "Remember, I've been put in charge to protect you, Detective."

Mrs. Janson returns just as Cynthia ponders her response. She looks at Al as the wife of the late Samuel Janson speaks.

Andrew, an employee at Samuel Janson's coffee shop in town, grasps his stomach and collapses while Cynthia and Al are interviewing him. *That could have been me*, she thinks, watching him wither on the floor. She's down next to Al holding Andrew.

"Oh my god!" says the clerk.

"Hurry, ma'am. Get me some cold water," Cynthia said.

"Dispatch—We have a thirty-three. Tell the boys to bring Prussian Blue for poisoning. Hurry, we're at—" Al looks up seeing the girl run for the phone.

"Yes, sir. They're five minutes away. Over and out—"

Andrew groans, "I feel... like I'm on fire."

"Can you tell me what you ate or drank in the last 24 hours?" Cynthia said.

"I had—" Andrew squirms.

Al pats Andrew. "Hang in there, buddy. Help's on the way."

———

Cynthia watches as Al talk with the paramedics. She comes up and flashes her ID while they're loading Andrew into the ambulance. "Thank God, you were here to save us, Big Al," Cynthia said as the ambulance pulls off.

"That's what I do."

"Our suspect knows we're on his trail."

"I believe so, Detective."

———

Nothing is ever that easy. The Investigative Unit went over every inch of the coffee shop but found no traces of thallium sulfate. Cynthia's team had spent hours going over the security footage, resulting in no new leads.

"So, I'm back to square one?" Cynthia's eyelids are beginning to feel like they're sticking to her eyeballs. "Time for a break." She turns to Al, who's been on patrol making sure no one except authorized staff enters. "I've looked over these case files for the fifth time today and still zilch," Cynthia said putting them inside her briefcase. "Boys, let's wrap this up in five."

"Ok, Ma'am."

"Big Al, let's go get something to eat and—?"

"And what?" He said glancing up at the clock.

Cynthia's tone was awkward. "Oh, I'm sorry for intruding. Maybe you have a date or two—"

"No, ma'am." Al touches her forearm. "I don't." She stares at him and Al said, "Unless you count my partner, Barry in. He's at home waiting for me to get off. He usually makes dinner for us."

Cynthia smiles, aware of Al's hand still resting on her arm while she clicks on her laptop. She should move, and let it drop, but she doesn't want it to move. The memory of Al's eyes earlier and promise to protect her has her mystified. Just as Cynthia starts to daydream, she lifts her hand to move the mouse on her laptop. Al's hand moves back. "I guess I'm in a threesome if Barry comes along."

"Oh my God! You have such a dirty mind. Barry's a home body. He's not coming."

"Don't mind me."

Cynthia shuts down her computer and Al gets up. "Let me give Barry a call and tell him I'll be late."

Cynthia sighs and folds her hands. "Now, who sounds like they're in a relationship?"

"No, he's just my roommate."

"Right—buddy."

Cynthia realizes that her thumb had been stroking where her wedding band used to be.

Al comes back into the room. "We're good."

"Great! Do you like pizza?"

———

Turns out Al doesn't like pizza, at least not the kind Cynthia was thinking of; quick slices on-the-go. He suggests a bistro named Janson's in town, with some of the best pasta Al claims he had tasted on this side of the Atlantic.

The place is more intimate than Cynthia expects; candlelights and couples lingering over glasses of wine. The place is nearly empty despite being dinner hour. Glancing over the menu, it's more pricey than Cynthia expected. "Maybe we should just get a couple of hot dogs and take them back to the station."

"Oh, come on," Al said looking over the menu. "If we did so, we'd waste hours in traffic."

"Well, unless your salary is three times more than a detective's, I think I'm going to have to order the—" Cynthia purposely picks the cheapest thing, "pasta e Fagioli."

"So cheap," Al said. "You must think I brought you here to spend all of your money. I'm here for a reason."

"What reason, Mr. Al?"

Al cuts his eyes toward a waiter a few tables over, pouring wine for a couple more interested in each other than their meal.

"The waiter? He's probably a college student working part-time. What do you think?"

"Why are you asking?"

Al shakes his head. "Never mind. Look at the manager over there near the kitchen."

"Whoa... did Samuel... rise from the dead?"

"Maybe." Al giggles. "The waiter is Samuel Janson's cousin, Bill. I had my boys look into Samuel and found them all here."

Cynthia closes the menu seeing the cover. *Janson's.* "I can't believe I didn't notice."

"I think someone wasn't happy in the family business."

"Maybe," Cynthia said. "Have you eaten here before?"

"No. But Barry told me the food is 'to

die for.' Let us hope he doesn't mean that literally."

The waiter starts walking toward them and Cynthia said, "Put the files away, Al. Hurry!" She pulls up her menu and pretends to read it.

"Actually, I want him to see these."

"Oh my God! No—"

"How are you folks doing this fine evening?" The waiter took out his pen. "Is this your first time at Janson's, sir?"

"It is, actually. I think I'll have some pasta but what do you recommend?" Al opens his menu beside the folder, marked with Samuel's name. "Or maybe I'll go with something with seafood in it?"

Cynthia watches Bill Janson out of the corner of her eye. His eyes widen when he sees the file and his hands are shaking. "Our baked ziti is some of the best in Manhattan, you can't go wrong there." He takes a step backward and glances back as if looking for an escape.

"I'm not sure what I want." Cynthia pulls out her badge and places it on the table. "Maybe we can talk about your best dishes back at the station."

Janson breaks and runs directly for the kitchen causing the patrons in the restaurant to yell. Cynthia pulls out her gun and her cell phone out at the same time, tossing the latter to Al. "Call for backup!"

Cynthia enters the kitchen yelling, "Freeze!" The kitchen staff is in shock as they come out one by one. Janson overturns a tureen and a cart and Cynthia fires off a warning shot. "Don't make this any worse, Mr. Janson!" Finding himself cornered, Bill grabs a knife from the rack and brandishes it.

"Drop it, Mr. Janson. It'll be a lot easier for you if you just come with me."

"Why?" He slashes with the knife and lunges. "You've already decided I'm guilty."

Cynthia's sure he's guilty now but she's

not going to be his judge or jury. She takes another step closer. "You can tell your side of the story at the station. We are good listeners."

Bill slashes again, and Cynthia moves backward. Her back hits the edge of a counter, and that gives Bill just enough room to slash at her hand. She moves it just in time but the gun goes flying and skitters under a stove. Cynthia stumbles trying to grab something - a pot, a pan, a tray - anything that will block him. Her hands close around something and it's heavy enough. She grabs it and hits Bill. "Fuck!"

The back door bursts open, and Al comes charging in. "No, Al—" Cynthia yells looking for her gun. Al tackles Janson to the floor but Janson still has the knife.

"Al! He's armed—"

Janson plunges at Al and Al twists out of the way, but not enough. The knife cuts through Al's coat and Bill loses the knife. As Al subdues Bill, Cynthia manages to kick the knife away. Bill's hands are now behind his back and he's handcuffed.

Cynthia is by Al's side. "Are you okay?" She yanks off her jacket and presses it against the wound now starting to stain his maroon waistcoat. Cynthia wanted to ask why Al didn't just wait for the damn backup, but she knows she owes him her life.

"It's not as bad as it looks." Al's blood is soaking through her jacket. "Cynthia, if I die, I—"

"Shh," she said. "No one's dying today." Not on my watch. Hang in there. The paramedics are on their way."

Cynthia presses harder, comforting Al until they arrive. She holds Al's hand as the paramedics work on him.

———

At the hospital, Cynthia stands by his side with his roommate, Barry.

"I'm so glad you made it through surgery in one piece," Cynthia said.

"I told you I'm here to protect you."

"Hey, Al. You're going to get yourself killed over a woman."

"For this one, I might."

"Stop it, Al. You're making me blush."

They chat for a bit and days later when Al's well enough, Cynthia doesn't ask him yet about what he was going to tell her.

CHAPTER TWO

Cynthia doesn't really hear it at first, she's detached from awareness barely feeling the covers above her. Someone's knocking.

Go away. Leave me alone. I'm enjoying this nothingness.

But someone knocks again. "Cynthia?" The voice slams her back to reality.

Her heart pounds, as the room's springs back to clarity. Still, she feels locked in the prison of her nothingness.

"Cynthia, please open the door. It's Al."

————

Three Weeks Ago

Cynthia's back at work and somehow it feels worse than the weeks Al was in the hospital. Not because she couldn't see him every day - she could, but because she couldn't work with him since he was assigned to desk duty.

She's lost track of the number of times she turned to Al to ask what he was going to say only to find Detectives Dustin and Liam or the Coroner Dr. Wesley interrupting. *She'll ask Big Al whenever she gets time.*

Cynthia sends Barry messages asking if Al is well enough to lead her detail again and Barry asks but Al tells him Captain Rowland hasn't given him the okay. The day Al is sent back as Cynthia's detail, he texts, "I'll meet you there."

"And—"Cynthia texts.

"I'll be there in twenty minutes."

"I guess," she texts back.

———

They're standing over the latest victim - an old woman who's sitting peacefully in front of her television. Al and Cynthia cover their noses at the stench of the corpse. Through his scarf, Cynthia says, walking around the armchair, "Our victim here could have passed away from anything. But do you see the ruddiness of her cheeks?

"Yes, I see them."

"Well, normally, the body after several days would turn blue. Call Dustin in here to check the kitchen."

"Yes, ma'am."

"There's no carbon monoxide here. All of the appliances run on electric," Dustin said. "I will get the guys to do a full inspection once you guys are finished." Dustin tilts his head at Cynthia gesturing she's ready to leave with Al.

"Ok, Dustin. Thanks, I'll take Mr. Sanchez with me to go pay a visit to one of her relatives."

"Detective, I'd like to ask for your permission to go back to the station."

"I already texted Rowland. She won't be needing you."

"Yes, ma'am—" Al puts his scarf back over his nose.

"I need you to give me a ride? I took a taxi over here."

"No, problem."

———

Cynthia watches Al as they head for his patrol car. He seems healthy. What's going on with him then?

"I'm doing better," Al said as when

Cynthia asks him. He's looking sideways as he drives. "Do you remember anything about that night?"

"Just a little. They put me to sleep in the ambulance. I'm just glad Janson didn't poke me in the heart."

"I'm glad, too. You were so fussy at the hospital. I thought they would keep you sedated."

"I was?"

"Yes, you were, Big Al."

Then there was a long silence.

Cynthia had stopped talking.

If she meets Al's eyes, she will kiss him. Al had saved her life again and Cynthia knew she owed him.

"I'm sorry," Al says after they've been on the road a while.

"What are you talking about, Al?" Cynthia sees Al's eyes on her, but she keeps hers on the road.

"I'm glad you were there—"

Her eyes break from the road. "I had to —" she says, turning her attention back. "It was a close call."

"Yes, it feels weird when one has suffered a loss one."

Even as Cynthia nods, she's reminded of his words before the ambulance came. "Al..."

"Yes, Detective?"

"Before, when you thought you were dying..."

"I nearly did."

Cynthia senses Al's trying to change topics. "What were you trying to tell me?"

"Ah." Al's gaze falls toward his hands. "I wanted... to tell you not to worry. That I would see you again."

"If you died, you'd see me again?" Cynthia laughed. "Where in heaven?"

"Maybe so or hell." Al reflects on what to say next. "You know my head wasn't on straight after losing all that blood. I just hoped to see you again."

"Okay, Al." Cynthia says under her breath, "I see I'm not going to get your confession today."

"What did you say?"

"Nothing, Big Al."

Cynthia has heard her share of deathbed confessions and getting the truth out of Al was going to be hard. "Well, I'm glad you're okay. Thanks for saving my life again."

"What are partners for?" Al shrugs and concentrates back on the road.

———

The autopsy on the old woman had come back. It wasn't what Dustin or Cynthia expected. The woman actually died from carbon monoxide despite not having gas appliances in her apartment. "This is a murder, then," Cynthia said balancing her phone on one ear as she types the victim's information into her laptop. "Penelope

O'Shea. There's not much on her: never been in trouble, married for thirty years before her husband died of a heart attack. No children, no significant assets, not even a car. "I can't imagine why anyone would want to kill an old woman as sweet as this lady."

"There's always a reason," Dustin says on the other line. "This was premeditated."

"Probably." Cynthia grabs her things. "Time to interview the neighbors. Do you want to come along?"

"I'm on my way." When Cynthia reaches her car, she realizes she hasn't called Al to accompany her. She texts him before starting the engine.

———

A moving van is out in front of the building when they arrive. Cynthia sees a woman looking onward while movers come in and out of the building. "Excuse me, ma'am.

May we talk to you for a second? This is Detective Dustin Holiday and I'm Detective Cynthia Cowens."

The woman frowns. "I'm Natalie Gaines. Is there something wrong?"

Cynthia looks at Dustin. "Did you know Penelope O'Shea, the old woman who died in this building?"

"Mrs. O'Shea?" The woman glances toward the third-floor window. "I saw her around, walking to the bodega on the corner in the mornings, doing things around the apartment building, but I didn't know her personally. Really sad that she passed away. Guess it was the old woman's time."

"Well, we are not convinced that it was yet," Dustin said. "We're here to investigate her murder."

"Murder? Oh, God!" The woman put her hands over her mouth. "Here? The crime rate's the lowest it's been in years."

"Well, murder can happen anywhere,

no matter how safe the neighborhood is, Ma'am," Cynthia said writing something on her notepad. "Do you recall anyone being close to Mrs. O'Shea?"

The woman thinks. "Ah—maybe Mr. Pak on the second floor? I saw them working on the rooftop garden together every start of spring." Her voice lowers. "I always thought they'd be perfect for each other, both widowed, around the same age..."

Cynthia's face blushes, thinking of Al. Do people talk about Cynthia and Al this way around the precinct? "She avoids looking at Al, but the woman gives Cynthia a cue about the hunk next to her. "Well, the two also used to play cards up there, when the weather was nice." The woman glances toward the roof. "It's really beautiful up there."

"Thank you, Ms. Gaines," Cynthia said after getting her details. "We might be in touch." Cynthia and Dustin head into the building, leaving Al outside to monitor the movers.

"This neighborhood is being gentrified. The shop on the corner Ms. Gaines is referring to is closer to a breakfast diner than a bodega," Dustin said as they stop in front of the first door on the second floor. No one comes to any one of the doors, no matter how loud they knock. "Perhaps Mr. Pak's already moved?"

"I think Ms. Gaines would have known that. She seemed to know a lot about both Mrs. O'Shea and Mr. Pak despite her claim of 'not really knowing' them personally."

Cynthia begins to walk toward the stairs. "I'll try again. Go see if you can find someone on the third floor who knows them?" She pulls out her phone as she descends the stairs.

"Ok."

After a few minutes of searching,

Dustin comes through with a name - Ned Hamilton - and a number. Cynthia calls while standing in front of a door. Whatever the reason, Ned doesn't pick up and Cynthia leaves a message. Ms. Gaines is on the first floor with the movers, who are finishing up.

"Al?" Cynthia calls down the stairwell. "Did anyone come in here?"

There's no answer.

"Al!" she yells. Is it really that hard to hear down there? Maybe he's busy speaking with someone.

Cynthia jogs downstairs, feeling something is wrong. Where is Al—the man who could get himself into trouble at a moment's notice.

Al's not in the hallway and looking around yields nothing. The sinking feeling doubles as Cynthia looks outside and doesn't see him on post. She goes back inside, stopping at every door to listen—still no Al. Suddenly, Cynthia remembers the rooftop garden. Maybe, he's up there.

"Dustin, come to the second floor. I can't find Al. I'm going up to check on Ned Hamilton."

"I'm coming—" His voice is faint on the line.

Cynthia then calls Ned's number. He doesn't pick up but Cynthia traces a phone ringing to an apartment on the second floor. "Hello?" She said banging on the door. "Mr. Hamilton? Are you in there?" The ringing continues, but Ned doesn't pick up. What is that smell?

Cynthia waits for Dustin to come down and then he kicks in the door. They see a middle-aged man on the floor. As they step inside, they're overwhelmed by the gas. They cough, stumbling back out into the hallway. "I'm going back in, Dusty."

"Wait."

Cynthia covers her face and goes back

inside. Dustin joins her and opens the windows, and then shuts off the stove. Meanwhile, Cynthia bends over to check Mr. Hamilton. He still has a pulse and is covered in blood from a bash to his head. A lamp is on the floor, broken in pieces. Someone did this, then turned on the gas to finish the job.

They can't stay there for long. Back in the hall, Cynthia calls 911. "We need paramedics now." Dustin goes back inside and pulls Mr. Hamilton out while Cynthia heads to check the other rooms, with her gun drawn.

The bedroom door is open. A man in on the bed with a gas mask over his face. Is this Mr. Hamilton's attacker?

Oh my God! It's Al.

Cynthia gasps and coughs. She goes to the window and opens it then kneels down to check on Al.

He has a pulse and no other signs of trauma. "Al? Al, can you hear me?"

There's no response at first but then he groans and rolls his head toward her "Cynthia?"

"Al, what are you—" Cynthia coughs again struggling to pick him up. She wants to say that Al is too heroic for his own good, acting like he has a death wish sometimes like he's some sort of superhero.

By the time she gets him up, Dustin comes back in and helps. They hear the sirens approaching. They lay Al down beside Mr. Hamilton, and his eyes flutter toward Ned. "It was him, he—" Al coughs and then says, "Handcuffs."

Dustin handcuffs the still-unconscious Mr. Hamilton, asking Al, "Did you knock him out?"

"I—" He coughs again. He levers himself up with a groan to a sitting position, one hand rubbing at his temples. "Call Barry, tell him Procedure Three."

"What?" Cynthia shouts. "Procedure

Three? The paramedics are right outside, Al, and they're taking you."

"Carbon monoxide—" He wobbles,"...can cause brain—" He sighs. "Can't work if—" Al slumps over groaning.

"Al!"

Dustin runs out to the hallway. "Up here, on the second floor!"

"Call Barry—" Al murmurs, and then there are several incoherent words. Cynthia leans in, to try to catch whatever Al's trying to say. "Need Barry now—don't worry—my Cynthia." He stops talking and she feels his lips brush her cheek.

Al passed out, but the paramedics are there, asking Cynthia questions as they take Barry and Ned downstairs. She calls Barry during the ambulance ride.

"Procedure Three, Al said. What's that?" Cynthia said.

"Ok. What hospital are you going to?"

"New York-Presbyterian."

"Ok, I'm on my way. I'll call backup. Thanks, Cynthia."

"What's Procedure—"

The phone hangs up. Cynthia doesn't even get an explanation. She stares at the phone, trying to hold on to the memory of Al's lips on her as if it will keep him alive.

CHAPTER THREE

The voice is distinct. Cynthia feels her mind playing tricks on her but it's a voice she desperately needs to hear again?

It doesn't matter. She finds herself walking across the hardwood floor as if in a dream, her fingers curling around the doorknob, and turning.

Cynthia regains her conscious in enough time to stop herself. This is madness.

In the past several months, she's learned to accept things that once seemed insane in stride. It was part of the rollercoaster ride of getting to know Officer Al Sanchez. She came to embrace it, the excitement of not knowing what awaited her day to day, making each new case an adventure.

But this? Hearing Al's voice on the other side of the door - a voice silenced forever - is beyond madness. Cynthia closes her eyes for a moment, takes a deep breath, and then pulls aside the door curtain to look.

Three Weeks Ago

She heads for the hospital as soon as possible the next morning, after staying with Al until she could barely stay up. His partner, Officer Barry put several bills into her hand, told her to get a taxi, go home and rest. Cynthia's thoughts are filled with images of shootings, drownings, car wrecks, stabbings and gas leaks. Every scene ends with Al Sanchez trying to tell her something - something important - and then he's gone before he can get the words out. She stares at the wall long before the first rays of sunrise across the window-dowpane.

Al had been sedated in the ambulance and then later in the hospital bed. As he lay there with an oxygen mask over his face, the doctor had tried being hopeful about his condition. Sanchez hadn't been exposed as much to the carbon monoxide as their murder suspect, Ned Hamilton, he told Cynthia. Hamilton had suffered severe brain damage from the gas - not head trauma, apparently, Al had hit him in just the right spot. Cynthia could fathom what was in the doctor's eyes when he was trying to soften the hard truths. He told her that Al could lose his memory. At any rate, when Al Sanchez wakes up - the doctor told her he couldn't say if Al would be able to work again.

———

A week goes by and it becomes routine that Cynthia checks in at reception at 7 AM and right as she gets off the elevator, there's Barry already there, carrying two paper cups of coffee. "Cynthia!" Glancing at the cups, he says, "Here."

"You drink. I've had enough coffee for the week." She looks at Barry hoping for good news. "Is he awake?

The usual answer is no but today there's something different.

"Yes, Barry's up."

"When?"

"A couple hours ago. The first thing he did was ask for you," Barry says, nudging her. "I was a bit afraid."

"How... how is he?"

"Oh, you know Big Al. He'll bounce

back." Barry jerks his head toward Al's room. "Come on, he'll be happy to see you - I was gonna make him wait to call you until after breakfast."

Cynthia walked into the room, not sure what she'll find. "Cynthia! You didn't have to come so early." Al closes his book and places it beside his half-eaten breakfast.

She looks at Barry amazed at Barry's quick recovery. "Are you kidding me?" Cynthia comes over to the side of the bed, placing her hand in Al's. "Of course, I was coming back right away. But Al, we've got to keep you out of the hospital."

"I agree," he says, while Barry adds, "Amen!"

Cynthia's a bit taken aback, they're both so chipper. "Has the doctor been by to see you?"

"Someone came by about a half-hour ago," Barry says, busying himself with moving a chair for her to sit in. He removes a towel from it. "They're saying it was a miracle that I survived."

"I know, Al."

"I'll undergo an MRI later this morning, and should be ready to go home soon." Al squeezes her hand. "I'm sorry that I keep putting you through all this."

"And after you promised!" Cynthia teases, not letting go. Her thumb traces little circles on his as if to make sure he's going to stay right here. "I'd say don't do that again, but I know you."

"Perhaps I shouldn't make those promises," Al says.

"Maybe."

———

Perhaps, he should go back to life in the Coroner's Office. After all, he's not a detective but was trained with the best. Cynthia should rely on Dustin more and Al less. She'd do it if it meant Al would stop putting himself in danger. But Cynthia had missed him, even more, when he was recovering from that stab wound, but she doesn't know if she can go through this again.

They've been quiet for several minutes. Barry slipped out, sensing that the lovebirds need this time alone. Cynthia won't let go of Al's hand pinpointing the moment Al had gone from mere colleague to friend. Now, he's become someone she cannot imagine life without.

———

Cynthia backs away from the revelation as her guilt begins flooding her. It has been only a year since she lost Kenneth. She knows that this is too soon, even though her body doesn't seem to agree. She gives Al's hand a light parting squeeze and then reaches for the chart hanging from the edge of the bed. Glancing at it, she asks, "So they've given you a clean bill of health?"

She smiles at the words at the bottom: The patient is expected to make a full recovery. She puts it back and something catches her eye at the last moment. "Wait... 'Alvareo' Sanchez?"

"What?"

She points to the name on the chart. "It says right here, 'Alvareo Sanchez.'"

Al's mouth opens. "How odd! I'll have Barry take care of it."

She hopes that's all it is - that they got his name wrong. What else could they have gotten wrong? His condition? "Maybe you should get a second opinion after you leave."

"I'm sure it's only a mistake" He stares at Cynthia. "If it would ease your mind, I will."

"Al... what does 'Procedure Three' mean?"

Al turns pale as he opens his mouth. But just then, a nurse comes in, bustling past Cynthia to go beside Al. "Finished with that?" she asks, pointing to the tray. "Not hungry, I see."

"I'm not big on breakfast."

The nurse chuckles. "You and half this floor. Well, you can get something you like better later." She holds up a finger to him. "But after you're gone, Mr. Sanchez. No more unscheduled strolls through the hospital."

"What?" Cynthia said looking at Al. This guy can't stop his shenanigans even here?

"Oh, yeah, we caught this one wandering the halls in the middle of the night, out of his hospital gown, with his coat on," The nurse said pointing at Al. "You've got an MRI in a few minutes. Stay put." She grabs heads out of the room, almost bumping into Barry coming the other way.

"I found a coffee shop with those bagels you like, Al."

"Did you know Mister Al went wandering last night?"

"What?" Barry shakes his head. "Did you sneak out when I was asleep?"

A weird look passes between them. "Yes, I did. I couldn't sleep and now I feel much better."

"Al!" Barry and Cynthia say together.

"Why not? I'm feeling better. No headache, my pain, and my head is on straight. I didn't feel like watching TV out of fear I'd wake you."

"Just because you studied medicine doesn't mean you can diagnose yourself!"

"Yeah... Mr. Alvareo," Cynthia said.

"Cynthia saw a mistake on the chart," Al says, sharing that odd look with Barry again. "She's sharp, even this early in the morning."

"Huh, well, we're getting you out of here the second that MRI is finished," Barry said. "They can't get anything right." Barry turns to Cynthia. "You should come and have lunch with us at my place."

"Well, I..."

"Come on," Barry says.

Cynthia looks over at Al. She's been avoiding getting close to anyone because the last time she did, she lost that person. The closer she gets to Al, the more she's almost lost him. Every sign points to turning in the other direction. But something about Al keeps drawing her in.

"Alright!"

The men smile and Cynthia says, "I'm cooking."

———

After just a quick call to Dustin and Rowland, she finds herself sitting beside Al in the back of a taxi. Barry had insisted on sitting up front. Once they're on the road, she nudges Al. "You sure you're feeling all right?"

"The doctors said I was fit to go home, didn't they?" His eyes stay on the passing buildings.

"Al, tell me the truth."

He turns toward her, then, taking her hand in his. "Alright, here is the complete and honest truth. I've never felt better than I do right now."

"Fine, Al, I believe you." Cynthia laughed it off. "You don't have to say it like that."

"Almost there, lovebirds!"

Cynthia smiles while Al caresses her hand.

———

"I can get out whatever you need," Barry said.

"Just let me have a look, and I'll let you know." She looks inside the cabinets and refrigerator. "Looks like you have everything I need."

Barry leaves out of the kitchen. "I'll leave you be. Think I'll go down to the shop and see if I can't scare up some customers." Cynthia is left with Al, at the table, with a book in his hand.

"I'll be fine here," she tells him. "Go rest and watch some TV."

"I'm fine here, too. I often sit here and read while Barry cooks." He turns a page.

Cynthia takes a bottle of olive oil from the pantry. "Is Barry the usual cook around here?"

Al closes the book. "I dabble sometimes... but Barry is the man."

"So you have a system here?" Cynthia fills a pot with water and adds salt and oil before turning the burner up to medium-high. "I guess you guys have been living here for years?"

"About five. Barry is like family."

"Maybe he is."

"Most of the time, we are but we have our issues sometimes."

"Oh?" Cynthia takes a mixing bowl from a cabinet and puts ground beef inside.

"Barry brought home the wrong tea again," Barry said after opening a cabinet.

"Well, that's family."

Cynthia and Al laugh enjoying this moment without a murder case hanging over them. She starts placing the meatballs into a skillet. "I can't imagine the two of you doing anything worse than bickering over who gets the obituary first."

"You'd be surprised. Once, Barry and I fought and our neighbor called the police on us."

Cynthia drops a meatball. "You, two—what was the argument about?"

"Well, it—" Al doesn't want to tell Cynthia everything. "Just a disagreement over some life decisions."

"I see." Cynthia puts the pasta into the boiling water thinking Al was not ready to open up to her.

Cynthia turns the meatballs and then sets down the spatula. "Everything looks good, smells good but—" She pauses. "Damn it!"

"What?"

"There's supposed to be garlic in the meatballs. Maybe I can put it in the sauce instead." Cynthia glances around the countertops, opening some of the cupboards.

Al gets close to her. "Let me." Without waiting for Cynthia to move out of the way, he reaches into a cabinet just above her head. His body is only inches away and she's enchanted by the smell of his cologne. His unshaven scruff on his cheeks and chin is so close Cynthia could run her fingers down it by simply lifting her hand. Her eyes are drawn to his long-lashed eyes and lips... She finds herself trapped, not being able to make her muscles obey.

Al pulls down a couple of garlic bulbs. "Here they are." He senses how close they are and how it would take so little movement to close the distance.

They hover there, not moving, not

speaking, barely breathing. He seems just as loath to move as she. The moment extends so long that Cynthia knows she has to move, to get out of the way or she will get in trouble.

It's Al who moves, his lips come down on hers, asking for consent. Cynthia pauses before conceding in. Al's lips move slowly waiting for her to take the lead. When she doesn't deepen, Al pulls back to look at her. His head tilts slightly, a non-verbal request for permission to kiss her again. As he waits, his eyes drift down to hers, as if he's hungry for more.

Cynthia pulls Al in. This time there is nothing gentle, there is no question of whether she's ready for this. She's been in denial for so long.

Al's hands encircle her, one climbing up to tangle in her hair and the other coming up to grip her shirt. His fingers brush her just below where Kenneth's ring hangs. That brief thought flits away as he presses her into the counter, one leg nudging between hers. The closeness, the sensation of it, makes her body thrum. Cynthia's insensate to anything but the pressure.

It's so strong that she almost doesn't respond to the bubbling sound of the pot boiling over. Al pulls away just as the flames leap from the pan.

"Oh my God!"

Al lunges forward to twist the burners to off, and the smoke alarm goes off. Cynthia covers her ears while Al snatches an oven mitt and covers the skillet and the pot. Cynthia sees flames licking up the side of Al's sleeve. "Al!" He steps back and pats out the fire with a kitchen towel.

There's shouting and the couple knows who is doing it. "What the hell have you done to my kitchen!?"

Cynthia looks at Al, he looks back, smokes in the air around them while the alarm is still blaring.

"Sorry, Barry."

"You know what—I don't even wanna know. I should have cooked myself. Get out of my kitchen!"

———

Al and Cynthia go in the living room, banned from entering the kitchen and just stares at each other. She's not sure who starts laughing first, but soon they both are.

The moment has passed, and Barry, Cynthia, and Al don't mention it for the rest of the day.

Cynthia gets a text while eating, "Looks like we have another dead one, Al."

CHAPTER FOUR

*A*l stands there, shivering from the morning chill, his eyes are bloodshot.

"Al, is that you?"

Cynthia unlocks the door.

"Al..."

It's really him, somehow, in the flesh. "Cynthia," he says, his voice breaks on the single syllable. "I—"

"How?" Her voice breaks. "I saw you—"

"It's—" he smiles. "It's a long story." He gestures inside her apartment. "May I?"

A Week Ago

Liam's voice is the first she hears as she enters the Coroner's Office. "Seems to be pretty cut and dry?"

She stays back, to listen to whatever Liam has to say but doesn't enter. Liam's bent over the deceased; one Oscar Warren, a doctor from the Upper East Side. Meanwhile, Al is back on duty and is by the door, looking on with his sweetheart.

"I mean, the bullet was shot at close range. Looks like a nine millimeter," Liam said. "I'd say a right-handed shooter based on the angle of entry, between five and six feet in height, and an amateur." He stops, waiting for comments. But when Cynthia remains silent, he says, "I mean, you're the Investigator in charge here. Wanna come closer?"

"I'm just taking it in," Cynthia cuts him

off. "You're correct so far. Go on. I'm listening."

"Glock 19, Generation Four," Liam adds. "One of the most sought after handguns in the black market." Al looks on smiling while checking out Cynthia's rear end.

Cynthia closes her eyes thinking more about Al than the deceased. It's been two weeks since the kiss in the kitchen, and neither one of them has wanted to bring up the subject.

She takes a deep breath and steps fully into the room. "What have you got for me?"

"Detective Jones!" Al says, turning. The subtle shift to using her last name instead of her first is a first.

"Officer Sanchez." Cynthia steps past Al. "Liam, you said something about a Glock 19?"

"Yes." Liam points to the bullet wound with his scalpel.

"Alright, so we have a murder," Cynthia says. "So?"

"It might be a crime of passion rather than a robbery."

"Was anything stolen?"

"Nothing."

"Well, when the report comes in—" Cynthia pauses while looking back at Al.

A memory of Al, shirtless in pain pops up. She's daydreaming while Liam is talking to her. Will she ever see Al again like this?

"Detective Jones?" Liam waves. "Are you here with me?"

Cynthia blinks and turns around from Al. "Yes, yes." She puts her hand on her head. "Just wondering about the victim. Dr. Warren wasn't married, right?"

"Maybe he was a 'playa.'" Al says from the door. "Maybe he never bought into the idea of settling down."

"Maybe," Cynthia says. Detective

Dustin comes into the room with Dr. Warren's credit card records.

"Thanks, Dustin."

"Al might be right. Most crimes of passion don't always stem from love gone sour. It could have been revenge... fear...disappoint."

"We'd better get going." Cynthia pulls Dustin. "Dustin and I will look into Warren and see what we can dig up. Thanks, Al for the tip."

"Certainly," Al said not reacting to her Cynthia's non-invite.

———

The longer Cynthia spends in Al's presence, the more questions come up. "I'll let you know if we need you for this one, Al."

"As you were."

Al nods and waves goodbye.

The farther Cynthia gets from the Coroner's Office, the quicker her steps are.

Just as she's reaching the doors, her cell phone buzzes. She stops but closes her eyes when she sees the name, Barry.

Can you come 'round to dinner tonight?

It's the fourth time he's invited her over since she almost set fire to his kitchen. Knowing how close he and Al are, she's sure Barry knows something, and now he wants to make up. Cynthia's ignored the texts but this time, she texted back.

"Not tonight, Barry. I just got a new case. Maybe some other time?"

"Ok. Don't be a stranger."

She pockets her phone and reaches for the door to push it open.

"Detective Jones?"

She turns around. It's Liam, jogging. "What, Liam? What is it now?"

"Oh, no," he says, bending over and breathing. "I'm glad I caught you. I thought I was going to have to chase you all the way to your car."

"I do have a phone, you know."

"Yeah, I know but I think it's better to talk about in person." Then he lowers his voice. "And away from your partner.'"

"What's going on?" Cynthia looks at Dustin. "Hey Dee, give us a minute. Matter of fact, I'll meet you at the squad car."

"Ok."

"I just wanted to ask... is there something going on with you and Sanchez?" Liam said.

Cynthia opens her mouth to try to deny it when he goes on, "I mean, just a couple weeks ago, you two were hitting it off."

"Liam, this is not the time."

"Okay, sorry."

"There's nothing to be. "

"Well, Sanchez is happy, everyone around the precinct is as well."

"I'm wondering why are you saying this

—" Cynthia glances to make sure Al doesn't come out and see them.

"You saw how Al was checking you out back there?"

"Yes. And—" she said, "Nothing is wrong with us."

"There is but you, two are acting like there isn't."

"Al has been going through a lot. I have too with all these crazy murders. That's all, Liam."

"Maybe—I wish you both just make love and call it a day."

"You're such a mess! I have to go. Bye!"

Once Cynthia in the driver's seat, she slumps forward, resting her head on the steering wheel.

"What's wrong, C?" Dustin said.

"I got a headache."

"Want me to drive?"

"No, just give me a minute."

———

"You were right about checking Mr. Warren's credit card records," Dustin says on the drive out. "Seems like he stayed at the Ritz Carlton and the Berring Park at least twice a week. Someone in the staff probably recognizes him."

"I hope so. It's too bad that no one seems to know what Warren did during his time off."

"Some people live in a cave," Dustin says. "I mean, you know I can't help talking about my wife and kids, but someone like Captain Rowland? As old as she is, I don't even know if she's married."

"She doesn't wear a ring, but that doesn't mean anything." Cynthia thinks of the ring on the chain around her neck and image of Al kissing her.

"Even Al. I mean, you see him all the time. Does he ever spend time with anyone outside of that jerk roommate of his?

Cynthia looks out the window as

Dustin keeps his eyes on the road. "As far as I know, Al's not seeing anyone."

Dustin laughs. "Sanchez's a bit of an oddball - maybe there's no one who will put up with him."

Cynthia feels offended but doesn't speak. Dustin sees the look on her face and apologizes. "I'm sorry, Cynthia, I know you two are—"

"Well, Al's a work in progress."

———

The hotel staff is pretty helpful telling Cynthia and Dustin that Warren was a good tipper and friendly. At the Ritz Carlton, he was seen regularly with a woman.

"Dr. Warren rarely came in with the same person twice," the receptionist says at the Berring Park, leaning in to whisper. "He was a big playboy."

"Never with the same woman, huh?" Cynthia said.

"Rarely. There were a few I saw more than once - a younger Asian girl, an older woman, and a middle-aged man in a suit. Dr. Warren didn't have a preference."

Dustin leans on the counter. "And they always checked-in?"

"Not always. Sometimes, Dr. Warren had drinks at the bar with the person he brought in, and left."

As they're walking away from reception, Dustin sighs. "That's gonna be a lot of footage to go through. You're thinking what I'm thinking?"

"Let's focus on the woman from the Ritz Carlton."

"Exactly." He glances behind him as they're exiting the front doors. "Bet Al would have nailed down the suspects before the receptionist finished her sentence." Dustin clears his throat before asking, "You wanna call him in on this one?"

"Think we can't handle this on our own?"

"No, that's not what I'm saying, I just, you know... wondered why Al isn't on detail with us."

"He's working his way back up." Cynthia tries to keep her voice low. "Maybe Captain doesn't believe he's fully healthy."

Dustin doesn't answer back until they get back to the car. "Cynthia, you'd tell me if there were something wrong, right?"

"There isn't anything wrong - other than a case that needs to be solved."

———

They spend the day tracking down their mystery lady and did so right before the dinner hour. "Andrea Villiers?" Cynthia says, knocking on the door. "Police. We need to ask you a few questions."

Ms. Villiers answers, wearing in a black cocktail dress, slipping on her heels. "Can I help you?"

"Ms. Villiers, we're looking into the

death of Oscar Warren. What was your relationship with the deceased?"

Ms. Villiers puts her hand over her mouth. "Death? Oscar's dead?" She steps back. "But we were going out this evening—"

"At the Ritz Carlton?"

"Yes," Ms. Villiers said.

Cynthia holds out her hand and Ms. Villiers takes it. "Would you like to sit down?"

Ms. Villiers nods and the two of them go over to the couch. "When... did Oscar die? How?"

"He was shot to death sometime last night, between 2 and 3AM," Cynthia said. "Were you seeing each other?"

"Oh my God!" Ms. Villiers puts her hand on her head. "Yes, he was my boyfriend."

"Were you serious?"

"I thought we were. We saw each other a few times a week. Sometimes he would come over here, sometimes we'd go out to the Ritz Carlton, or just take a drive."

While Cynthia is talking with Ms. Villiers, Dustin is walking around the apartment, observing anything unusual.

Ms. Villiers trembles and Cynthia takes a blanket off the couch and places it around Ms. Villiers's shoulders. "Can I get you some water?"

"Yes, please."

Cynthia pours water, and out of the corner of her eye, she sees Dustin opening and closing drawers, looking for evidence. She then hands her the glass, and Ms. Villiers takes a sip.

Dustin fishes out a Glock 19 from a drawer between two gloved fingers. "Ms. Villiers, does this belong to you?"

Ms. Villiers turns. "Yes, my father gave it to me as a present. He told me I should have it because of the crime in the city." Then she seems to realize why Dustin is asking. "But I didn't kill Oscar!"

"You won't mind if we run ballistics on it." Dustin bags it. "Where were you last night between 2 and 3AM?"

"In-in bed, like I usually am." Her hands tremble, the water in the glass sloshes.

"You have anyone who can verify your whereabouts at that time?"

"That won't be necessary. I know Ms. Villiers."

"Al, what are you doing here?" Ms. Villiers says.

Everyone turns to see Al at the doorway. He steps inside, nodding to Cynthia and Dustin. "How did Al know we were here? Dusty—" Cynthia murmurs.

"Ms. Villiers's gun could have been used for the crime but is she the shooter? Remember the murderer was right-handed."

Cynthia looks at Ms. Villiers's hands, cradling the glass, right hand over left.

"In fact, we went to school together."

Al continues, "I'm sure she's not responsible." Al walks up to Dustin and holds out his hand.

"I'll call Ballistics down here."

———

Within thirty minutes, Dustin has verified the gun wasn't the murder weapon. Ms. Villiers said she hasn't had anyone over since Oscar came by last weekend. Cynthia watches as Al and Dustin assure her that she'll be protected. With a light touch on Ms. Villiers's arm, Cynthia stands, taking her phone from her pocket. She points to it, and then out the door into the hallway. Dustin nods, but Al doesn't seem to notice.

When Cynthia's out in the hallway, she sighs, "I'll let you boys handle the rest."

"Need a ride, C?"

"I'll take a taxi back."

She steps outside to wave a taxi down

when someone says, "Detective? Detective!"

A taxi pulls up.

"Cynthia!" Al says, appearing beside her. "Please, let me drive you back."

"Wesley Heights," she tells the taxi driver before turning back to Al. "I'm Detective now? What do you want?"

"Let me apologize. Dustin had asked me to come down just in case—"

"Well, here you are. Thank you once again. You're not dead at least. Now, I'm going to go home."

Al stops her putting his hand on her arm. "Cynthia..."

"The meter's running."

"Then let me hop in with you."

She pauses, looking down at his hand on her arm, its warmth and pressure reminding her of why she's needed a break from him. Then Cynthia looks up. There's a yearning there, stronger than she's ever seen. Despite that, she knows that if she tells him to go, he will. She opens her mouth to say that and while doing so, her eye catches a figure walking toward Villiers's apartment building. Al's eyes follow hers. "It's that guy a suspect?"

Cynthia walks up to the taxi driver, tossing a twenty dollar bill in his lap. "Sorry, it looks like I'm staying."

———

Unholstering her gun and placing it in her coat pocket, the two walk back toward the building. Cynthia calls Dustin but it goes to voicemail. "Hey, Dustin," she says at the tone, "A man just entered the building, about 5'8", black hair, think he might be after Ms. Villiers."

"That's Tim Rust," Al whispers. "From the Berring Park Hotel. I know him. We went to school together, too."

"God, Al! You went to school with everyone today."

"That weasel, Tim Rust, was a criminal in third grade. I head him off before he gets to Ms. Villiers's if that's where he's headed."

"No, Al. Let me handle this."

"I'm here to protect and serve."

"Cut the bullshit, Al. You're going to get yourself killed." Cynthia radios in the precinct. "Possible murder suspect, Tim Rust, on the loose. Be advised. Present location - Ms. Villiers' apartment.

"Over and out, we're heading to your location now, Detective."

Al follows and at the stairs, Mr. Rust notices them behind him and smiles. Cynthia smiles back, threading her arm through Al's looking like a couple on the way home. Her other hand stays in her pocket, fingers curled around the trigger.

They let Mr. Rust get a little farther ahead to allay his suspicions. He leaves the stairwell to go to Ms. Villiers's floor and pulls a set of keys as he walks. Cynthia looks toward Ms. Villiers's door. Where is Dustin? Still inside the apartment with Ms. Villiers?

Mr. Rust turns his head to look behind him again. Cynthia pretends to be in her own little world, squeezing Al's arm and leaning in to whisper in his ear giggling. "Act natural."

Al turns to whisper in her ear as well. But Mr. Rust panics, swiveling toward them and pulls out a gun. "Get back!"

Cynthia and Al draw their guns. "Tim Rust? Police! Drop your weapon!"

"No, you drop your fucking weapon," Mr. Rust says shaking. "I'm gonna get away... or else."

Cynthia takes steps toward him, hoping to calm him down. "Just lower your weapon, Mr. Rust. All we want to do is ask you a few questions."

"He was mine," Tim murmurs, twitching on the handle of the gun.

The door to Ms. Villiers's opens, startling Mr. Rust. His gun goes off and the bullet goes wildly off to the right. Then he turns to point at the door.

Bang!

Rust drops to the ground, and his gun falls out of reach.

Cynthia risks looking behind her as she approaches Mr. Rust. She expects to see Al lying bleeding on the floor, considering his track record. But he's securing the scene calling in backup.

What she sees in the doorway is not Dustin, but Ms. Villiers. A curl of smoke rises from the end of the barrel held rock steady in her hands. Then she crumples to her knees, lowering her weapon.

Dustin comes running from the back of the apartment, huffing. He pries the weapon from Ms. Villiers. "All clear."

"How did you get that weapon, ma'am? I took it from you earlier," Dustin says.

"I have two; the one you have and another in the front, just in case."

"Are there more guns in the house?"

"No, sir."

Cynthia squats beside Tim. He's dead, a clean shot through the heart. Before she can call for Al, he's with her on the other side of Tim. "I think Mr. Rust matches our profile for the murder," Dustin says picking up another Glock 19 that fell feet away from Tim.

Al and Cynthia ride in silence. It doesn't seem to matter if Al is included or excluded - she can't protect him. He's going to get himself into trouble no matter what. So she has a choice. And she'd rather have him by her side, where she can keep an eye on him. Cynthia glances over at Al, at the way the passing lights are reflecting off his face.

"So—" Cynthia says, "we can't put this talk off much longer."

"I'm sorry," he says, eyes flinching away. "I shouldn't have kept you waiting."

"You're sorry?"

"Yes." Al studies his hands as if he's afraid to look at her. "I believe I was - how did Barry put it? - 'freaked out.' It's just been so long since I have been in something like this."

"So, there have been others," Cynthia says, "Like Iona. And then there's all the... equipment... in your basement."

"Just a gym rat. That's all." Al licks his lips before continuing, then finally turns back. "I needed to be sure this is what I wanted."

"And—" Cynthia licks hers. "Is it?"

He takes one of her hands in his, and her palms are sweaty. "I do if you do."

The fear of losing Al, just like she lost Kenneth, keeps latching onto her soul and whipping her around before she can take that final step but today is different. "I want it."

Cynthia comes forward, her hands skim over Al's police jacket to grasp the lapels. She pulls him closer, not worried about what the taxi driver will think - he's seen much worse in his career than two adults making out in the back seat. She wants to do much worse, to make up for the two weeks of dithering that seems silly now. But it will have to wait.

Her hands slide below his jacket, her fingers playing across his back to touch as much as him as she can. His fingers are drawing designs across her blouse, up into her hair, with more kisses.

Al's touch is starting a fire, fanning sparks to flames - welcome ones, unlike the fire in his kitchen. She shifts in the seat, bringing one leg up and over his to half-sit in his lap, never breaking the kiss. Al groans saying, "Cynthia," before beginning a trail of kisses down her neck.

Cynthia closes her eyes and relaxes her tongue inside his mouth. She groans and shifts, grinding on him. She can feel his cock against her; planted, bulging almost erupting.

The car slows down and the driver clears his throat. "We're here, ma'am."

"Sorry!"

Cynthia climbs from Al's lap, pulling her purse from the floor to pay. She glances at Al, his police jacket is riding up exposing his white shirt. "Let me pay."

"No, I got it," She pays and the couple gets out.

"Do you want to come inside? Have a cup of coffee? Maybe continue where we left off?" Al says as he opens her door.

"The latter sounds better," Al rubs her as he speaks, "I think we have much to discuss."

Cynthia can't get the money out fast enough to pay the driver.

CHAPTER FIVE

Al is there, asking for permission to enter. It is like he's a vampire. Cynthia nods and takes a step forward, to feel Al, to see if he's real.

She's drawn to him, like a magnet - and her touch turns into a hug. He's warm, definitely real. She gives into the craze, pulling him in tighter.

"Oh, Cynthia," he says playing with her hair, "the last thing I wanted to do was cause you pain."

Al then releases. He touches her cheeks and runs down the tracks of tears. "I should have told you," he says. "Long before this ever happened."

"What are you saying, Al?" Cynthia can't break the spell.

"How I knew what my ending would be."

———

Last Night

It's Dustin's that wakes her. "Cynthia? Cynthia, are you okay?" "Hurry with the paramedics. We may have casualties."

Her vision starts to clear. She nods but stops herself and shakes it 'no.'

"What happened?"

"There was a blast." Dustin squats beside Cynthia who reaches down and life one of the pieces of shrapnel. There is no sign of Al."

"Oh my God! Look at Barry. Where's Al?"

Cynthia whips her head toward the living room to see paramedics bending over Barry's body. His eyes are closed and he's shaking.

"They're working on him," Dustin says. "He's alive - looks like he got hit in the head pretty badly. Cynthia, you're bleeding. What the hell happened?"

She closes her eyes for a moment. "There was a package delivered. When Al put it in the chair, we heard a hissing sound. Al grabbed it and ran. That's all I remember. Where's Al?"

"It looks like you were targeted—we can't find him," Dustin says.

"Where is he? He can't be just gone."

"I don't know."

Dustin pats her on the shoulder. "We'll find him." He holds out his hand to help her up. "You're hurt. We need to get you to the hospital."

"No, I can't leave without Al." Cynthia

pulls herself up, using the arm of the sofa as leverage. "Al, Al—"

"Cynthia, we have to go".

She feels his hands on her shoulders. "Dustin, don't let IU touch anything."

"Ok. They won't until you go through it first. We have to go now."

Lowering her hand, she turns to face him. "Dustin, where's Al? I need to find out where he is?"

"We'll find him. I know."

Cynthia concedes.

"Don't touch anything. Bring every last envelope to the fucking precinct!"

———

Instead of going to the hospital, Cynthia heads to the precinct with Dustin. Boxes are brought in one by one piling up on her desk. She feels that Al had left a secret - and she cannot permit anyone else to see them. Although Cynthia can't explain it, her gut feeling is that Al's secret and his disappearance are connected.

After her hasty repacking, whatever system Al had is in shambles. A journal from the 1800s mixed with newspaper clippings from the 50s. Underneath photos and drawings without any date at all and notes in Al's handwriting. There are many references to death; different types, covering over a hundred years. Some horrific, some mundane. Al has always considered himself a student of death; she had no idea how far it went. Still, these leads were far-fetched.

"Detective Jones." Captain Rowland's voice startles her.

Cynthia looks up, pushing her hair behind her ears. "Yes, Captain?"

Rowland pauses. Cynthia hadn't cared what she looked like after the blast. What are a few cuts when Al's missing?

"Go home."

"But Captain, Al is—"

"I know. Detective Dustin filled me in. The FBI was called in to assist. They're doing everything they can. Al will be found, Detective."

"No, I can't just give up like this. He's my—"

"Detective, you look like hell and can't do your work in this state." Cynthia steps forward. "It's midnight. Go home, get some sleep. We have this covered."

"Captain—"

"Do I have to give an order?"

Cynthia shakes her head and places everything back in the box. Rowland watches her, waiting until she's left the precinct. Though Cynthia doesn't turn around, she feels a uniformed officer watching her until she gets into a squad car and it pulls off.

She replays the night's events... until someone knocks on her door at 3 AM.

"Detective, we've found Al," An officer said.

"Where is he?"

"He was burnt badly and didn't make it."

"Where was the body found?"

"A few feet from the fire escape. He almost made it."

ACKNOWLEDGMENTS

Thanks for reading and please leave a review. This will really help us out.

Consider joining our mailing list by sending us a hi at therealjustbae@gmail.com. We give out FREE Audiobook codes all the time.

Join our IG page here: instagram.com/justbaebooks

Join our FB page here: facebook.com/authorjustbae

Best of regards,
Just Bae